Pets

Written by
Jill Atkins

Some pets live in cages.

Hamsters, mice, guinea pigs, rabbits and birds live in cages.

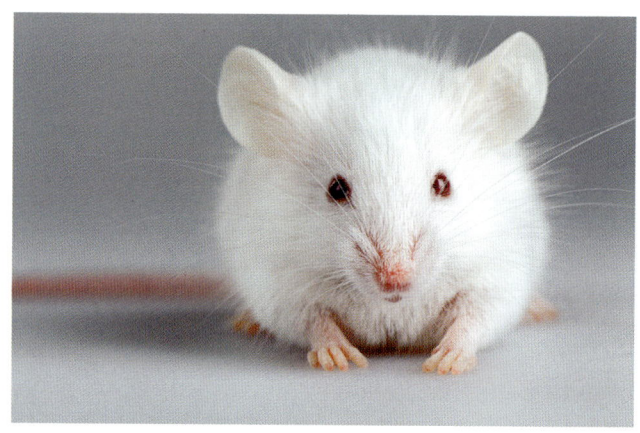

Inside their cages, they need a dish for their food and a water bottle.

Some pets live in tanks.

Newts and fish live in tanks.

Inside their tanks they need fresh water, weed, rocks and food.

Some pets live in houses.

Dogs and cats live in houses.

Cats like to stay snug and warm.

Dogs need to go for a walk every day.

Some pets live outside.

Horses and tortoises live outside.

In winter, horses live in a stable and eat hay.

In winter, tortoises need to sleep.

Do you have a pet?